Ruby and the Magic Stones

PRAISE FOR *STORYSHARES*

"One of the brightest innovators and game-changers in the education industry."
– Forbes

"Your success in applying research-validated practices to promote literacy serves as a valuable model for other organizations seeking to create evidence-based literacy programs."
- Library of Congress

"We need powerful social and educational innovation, and Storyshares is breaking new ground. The organization addresses critical problems facing our students and teachers. I am excited about the strategies it brings to the collective work of making sure every student has an equal chance in life."
– Teach For America

"Around the world, this is one of the up-and-coming trailblazers changing the landscape of literacy and education."
- International Literacy Association

"It's the perfect idea. There's really nothing like this. I mean wow, this will be a wonderful experience for young people."   - Andrea Davis Pinkney, Executive Director, Scholastic

"Reading for meaning opens opportunities for a lifetime of learning. Providing emerging readers with engaging texts that are designed to offer both challenges and support for each individual will improve their lives for years to come. Storyshares is a wonderful start."
- David Rose, Co-founder of CAST & UDL

Ruby and the Magic Stones

Lori Werhane

STORYSHARES

Story Share, Inc.
New York. Boston. Philadelphia

Published in the United States by Story Share, Inc.

The characters and events in this book are fictitious. Any similarity to real persons, living or dead, is entirely coincidental.

Storyshares
Story Share, Inc.
24 N. Bryn Mawr Avenue #340
Bryn Mawr, PA 19010-3304
www.storyshares.org

Inspiring reading with a new kind of book.

Interest Level: Middle School
Grade Level Equivalent: 3.3

9781642611786

Book design by Storyshares

Printed in the United States of America

Storyshares Presents

1

Her hair was a blondish, brownish mess on top of her head. She wore jeans that were a tad too short. On her feet were canvas high tops in a black and white zebra pattern. They were tied loosely, with one pink and one green shoe lace. She always wore a big, blue parka with a hood over her head. Her backpack had all kinds of small toys attached to it. They clanked and clinked as she swayed down the sidewalk.

Her name was Ruby. She was twelve and a bit of an odd girl.

It was cold, one day, as Ruby walked to school. She looked at all the kids coming and going but never really looked AT them. Some said hello, some glanced away, and some even knew her name. Ruby turned her head down when this happened and often had no idea how or why anyone would know who she was.

The other kids were never mean, but they weren't nice either. If an adult was close by, they would smile and give Ruby a *hello* or a nod. But, if it were just her and a bunch of kids, they mostly ignored her.

When Ruby arrived at school, she walked to the far corner of the building. She passed a sign that said "Special Education" and headed into the room. In her head, she thought, *Ugh, I don't want to try today.*

You see, school—well, learning—was difficult for Ruby. She worked really hard every day to get through her lessons. She was miserable.

She sat down and pulled her hood over her ears.

OMG, so loud, SO loud, she thought. *I cannot concentrate! Why is it always SO loud?*

This was pretty much how each day at school went for Ruby. Overwhelming . . . loud . . . not a lot of fun.

2

Finally, the day was over! Ruby exhaled and walked toward the door. On her way home, she looked down and watched her crazy shoes scrape, thud, scrape, thud—until something pulled her gaze away. She glanced over to the grass and saw a small bag. Ruby turned to see who else was nearby before heading towards it.

It was a red velvet bag that was small enough to fit in her hand. She picked it up and noticed that it was warm—even though the air was cool. She put it in her pocket and headed home.

Once she was safely in her bedroom, she closed the door. She grabbed the bag and went to the far corner of her top bunk to examine it. Inside were four shiny stones—not the kind you find on the street but smooth stones of all colors. Green, blue, red and yellow—some with gold and silver flecks. They were beautiful.

3

As Ruby examined the rocks, she noticed that the green one had begun to glow. She put the others to the side and picked up the glowing stone between her fingers. It was warm. She closed both hands around it, and the heat of the stone traveled through her whole body, until she couldn't sit up anymore. She closed her eyes and felt as if the stone grew into a giant, heavy boulder that lay on her chest. The weight felt so good, though. Her brain was calming down. Her entire body felt at peace.

What is this green stone? she wondered.

As she drifted off to sleep, she felt someone touching her shoulder. She looked up and saw a large, green . . . something. *Is it a nose, a cheek?* She couldn't tell.

"Hello?" she said quietly.

"Oh, hello you," the something said.

Ruby blinked twice to clear her eyes and could not believe what she saw. A huge, beautiful creature with green skin and hair stood before her.

"Who are you?" Ruby asked.

"Oh, there you are. You found my stone. That means you needed me. I am a Glindle—a fairy that can only be seen by those who touch my glowing stone. When a child in the human world experiences life very intensely, they need me. I sort out all the noise in your head, so you can see and feel what is important," the fairy said.

"What is your name, uh, err . . . what should I call you?" Ruby asked.

"Gwendolyn is my name, dear Ruby," she answered.

"How do you make it quiet for me?" Ruby asked.

Gwendolyn explained that the green stone, when close to Ruby, would calm the world around her. As long as she kept it close, it would help her brain sort out the noise and find what was important.

Ruby looked down at the glowing stone, closed her eyes, and woke up in her bed at home.

4

The next day as she walked to school, she held her hand over the pocket where the green stone sat. She could feel the warmth and the weight of it. Other children passed her, but they had no idea she carried something special with her. Weird Ruby looked just the same to them.

As she entered the hallway to her classroom, she felt different. It was not as loud. The other kids were not as crazy as before. She could make sense of all the conversations around her without feeling upset. She even looked up, made eye contact, and returned a hello to another student. *What is different today?*

She took her seat, took off her coat, and placed the green stone in the front pocket of her jeans. For the first time ever, she felt good being at school. The green stone was like a heavy blanket, surrounding her all day. She smiled, worked, laughed, and actually enjoyed her lessons.

"Hey Ruby," she heard.

"Uh, yeah?" Ruby responded.

"Ruby, it's Lizzy. What's up?"

"What?" asked Ruby.

This had never happened before. Lizzy lived two houses away but had never spoken to her. *Or, maybe she has, and I didn't notice.*

Something had changed in Ruby's brain. All of a sudden, other kids were starting to slow down and make sense to her.

"Ok, well, whatever. But, hey, do you, like, want to walk home together?" Lizzy asked quietly.

"Oh, um, ok," Ruby said, completely blown away.

So she and Lizzy did. They didn't talk a lot, but at least Ruby felt like she could hear her. They both had dogs, both liked dipping their french fries in chocolate shakes, and they both had crazy high-top shoes. *How have I never noticed that before?*

When Ruby got to her house, she said to Lizzy, "Uh, bye, see you tomorrow?"

"Cool, maybe we can hang out?" responded Lizzy, while she walked toward her house.

Weird, thought Ruby. She held onto the green stone, looked up at the sky and whispered, "Thank you, Gwendolyn."

5

That night, Ruby crawled into bed and dug out the magic bag of stones. She wondered about the other stones and whether they had certain abilities too. Sure enough, as she opened the bag, the blue stone began to glow. She pulled it out with her fingers and lay it on her belly as she looked up at her ceiling.

A tingling sensation took over her whole body. It was as if she were being petted by a hundred tiny hair brushes. First, it felt strange. Then, it felt calming. She fell asleep with the blue stone still sitting on her belly.

When she awoke, she found herself in a warm pool of bright, blue water. It felt amazing as she floated freely. She looked up and saw a large, blue creature floating above her. It had wings that were as wide as a school bus. She watched it glide and float in a very peaceful way.

"Who are you?" Ruby asked.

"Hellllllooooooo," the creature said very slowly. "My name is Bradley, and I am a Bindle. You are here because my special blue stone lit up around you. You must have a brain that is slow to find math skills. You see, I bring the magic of memory speed to you when you need it."

Ruby remembered that math was especially hard for her, but she never understood why. She did know she could never seem to recall how to start a problem. And she definitely couldn't remember her multiplication tables. She had always hated math because she was terrible at it.

Maybe Bradley can help me just like Gwendolyn has? Ruby closed her eyes and went under the water. When she came up, she was in her own bed.

6

Ruby jumped out of bed and began to get dressed for school. She carefully put the green and blue stones in the front pocket of her jeans. As she walked out her front door, she looked up and saw Lizzy.

"Hey, wanna walk with me?"

"Ok," Ruby answered. Together, the two girls walked and talked until they got to school.

"Ruby, can I ask you something?" asked Lizzy, when they arrived.

"Sure."

"Why do you always go to the stupid kid room?" Lizzy asked and then stopped. "Uh, I mean, Special Ed?"

"I've always gone there. I think my brain is weird or something. Up until yesterday, I thought school was the loudest place on Earth. But lately something has changed in me," Ruby tried to explain.

The girls parted ways, and Ruby headed toward her classroom. She walked in and, like yesterday, the room was quiet. The green stone felt warm in her pocket, and she felt like a heavy, warm blanket was wrapped around her.

The blue stone was different. It hummed and rumbled in her pocket. She felt a soft vibration all over.

As she sat in her seat to start a math assignment, Ruby felt her brain wash away. The page of multiplication problems seemed clearer today.

Five times five is . . . twenty five, Ruby thought. *Did I know that yesterday?*

Four times two is . . . eight, she thought. *Wow, I actually know that too.*

She continued to work on the math sheet for another few minutes until it was done. That, too, had never happened before. She found herself raising her hand and answering her teacher's questions. She didn't cry or put her head down in frustration.

The magic stones were transforming her life.

Is this what it feels like to be a normal kid? she wondered. *'Cause school is lot easier than it ever was before.*

The bell rang, and she sprinted to the front door to find Lizzy. She was standing in a group of kids who all turned toward Ruby.

"Oh, hey Ruby . . . this is Carly, Mary, and Kelly," Lizzy said, while pointing to each girl in turn. "Wanna walk home with us?"

"Sure," said Ruby. "Hi, everyone."

The girls walked out the door and headed for home. Ruby smiled as she placed her hands over her pockets.

She felt the blue stone resting there, and she quietly thanked Bradley for being with her that day.

7

Ruby was beginning to feel like a new kid. She was happy, instead of tired all the time. She was making new friends. Life felt so good.

That night, she crawled into bed and reached again for the magic bag. This time, the red stone glowed, begging to be picked up. Like the others, it was warm to the touch. She placed the stone on her forehead. It seemed to just want to be there, so she gently held it above her eyes.

The stone lit her entire room up with a warm, red glow. Instantly, her eyes closed, and she fell into a sound, sound sleep.

When she awoke, she realized she was surrounded by warm, smooth stones. Thousands of small stones cradled her in a sitting position. She felt very comfortable and safe.

She heard a slow clicking sound and noticed a large, red tortoise-like creature walking toward her.

"Hello, I'm Ruby," she said.

"Oh, hello there. I am Rosey. I am a Rindle. My glowing, red stone brought you to me. My magic connects all the thoughts in your head to your hands."

"I'm not sure what you mean," Ruby said.

"My magic, red stone helps you to write - a lot!" Rosey explained.

Ruby remembered how the other stones had helped her to find her strengths, too. *Maybe it was possible that she could actually write well!* She rubbed her eyes, yawned and fell fast asleep.

8

Ruby woke up early the next morning. This had never happened before. Usually, her mother had to wake her up many, many times for school. Then she would usually throw on whatever she could find and stumble out the door.

This morning, she had time for a shower. She carefully brushed her hair and teeth and put on a little lip gloss. She found some clean clothes in her closet that actually matched and fit. Then she placed the green, blue, and red stones in her front pockets.

Well, I guess I'm not that weird, she thought, as she laced up her zebra high tops. *Some things are never too crazy to wear!*

Out the door she went to find Lizzy and the other girls waiting.

"Ruby, looking good!" said Mary.

"Girl, you're looking amazing," added Lizzy.

"Thanks, I guess I just lucky today," said Ruby, as she smiled and walked, looking up at the sun.

The girls giggled and talked on the way. Ruby had never noticed how amazing the warm sun felt on her cheeks before.

"I think this is going to be a great day!" she announced.

"Totally!" screamed the other girls.

Once at school, Ruby entered her classroom. It was still quiet, but something was different. Her teachers were looking at her.

"Wow Ruby, you look so cute today," Ms. Thomas said with a smile. "And you are doing amazing work this week. We have all noticed."

"Thanks," said Ruby, "I feel good too." She sat down at her desk, patted her front pockets and got to work. That day, she had to write a story.

Strangely, ideas came to her quickly. She took her pencil and began writing and writing and writing.

Usually, she would write a sentence or two and her pencil would break. Then she would drop it, pick it up, twirl it, sharpen it, and finally, forget what she was writing. Not today, though. Today was different.

Her ideas were clear, thoughtful, and on the paper! It felt so natural, so easy. Again, she thought, *is this how school is for other kids?*

Ms. Thomas came up behind her and picked up the paper. "Ruby, you've been busy!" As her teacher read her story, Ruby noticed a tear coming down Ms. Thomas's cheek.

"What's wrong?" asked Ruby.

"Oh, nothing is wrong. I am so proud of you! It's as if a door has been unlocked in your brain this week. It is so amazing to see what you can do," said Ms. Thomas. "I think I'm going to keep this and show it to a few people. Maybe it's time for you to think about visiting a general education classroom?"

"Really?" said Ruby. "Can I do that?"

"Oh, yes, you can and you should," said Ms. Thomas, "I will talk to a few teachers and maybe tomorrow we can sit in on a few classes and see what you think."

"Wow, ok, I think I can do that," whispered Ruby. She put her hands over her magic stones and added, "Thank you, Rosey!"

That night, she went home and went straight to her room. She climbed back up into her top bunk and held her magic stones in her hand. *Could it have always been this easy to unlock my brain? A few magic stones?*

And the bag still had one more stone in it.

Ruby wondered what new gift it would bring to her.

9

The yellow stone looked like a little sun inside the bag. Ruby pulled it out and placed it on the blankets in her bed. The gold flecks glowed darker as the stone warmed the air around her. Ruby decided to pick it up and hold it close to her heart as she slept. The heat from the stone filled her chest with a strange sensation. She wasn't quite sure what it was, but it felt really good.

When she woke, she was being carried. She looked up and saw a beautiful, yellow animal holding her.

"What are you?" she asked.

"I am a Spangle. My name is Sunny and you have obviously come across my magic, yellow stone."

Ruby replied, "Yes, I did. How do you help me?"

Sunny explained the yellow stone was one of the most powerful to exist. It would give Ruby's brain the ability to read and understand at the same time. The yellow stone would give her the power to love books! And that would open up so many other gifts as well.

"But I hate reading. I have never read anything I liked. I'm not sure if I believe the yellow stone has all the power you think it does," Ruby said.

"Just wait, my dear. Just wait!" Sunny said with a smile.

10

The next morning, she woke up early again for school, got dressed, placed her magic stones in her pockets and met the girls on the curb.

"What do you think about the book we are reading in Language Arts?" asked Kelly.

"Yuck, it's so weird. I don't get it," said Mary.

"I kind of like it," said Lizzy.

"A girl getting notes, like from some future guy . . . it is weird, but I kind of like it, too," said Carly.

Ruby thought to herself, *books—yuck!* She had never liked to read . . . anything!

"Hey, Lizzy, I think I'm coming to your Language Arts class today. You know, just to watch," said Ruby.

"Do you think you'll get to come every day?" Lizzy asked. "That would be awesome!"

"I don't know . . . just today for now," said Ruby.

"Well, it will be so cool to see you during the day," said Lizzy.

The other girls nodded in agreement as they reached the school.

Ruby got to her classroom, took off her coat and patted the magic stones in her pockets. Ms. Thomas came right up to her and said, "Are you ready? Don't worry, I'll be in the room just in case you need to leave, but I feel good about this!

Ruby exhaled, looked up at the ceiling and felt the warmth of her pockets. *I got this!*

Ms. Thomas and Ruby went to Lizzy's Language Arts class. They walked in and found an empty desk near the back.

"Ok class, we were discussing the book *When You Reach Me*," said Mr. Monroe, from the front of the class.

One of the kids passed a paperback to Ruby. She touched the cover and read, *When You Reach Me* by Rebecca Stead.

I dont know. I've never been able to read a book without getting confused or bored, thought Ruby. Just then, the yellow stone in her pocket burned her just a little bit. *Ouch!*

She picked up the book and started reading. And reading and reading and reading until she heard the bell ring. *She HAD to finish this book! How did it end? Would they all be okay in the end?*

Never before had a book grabbed her attention so much.

Ms. Thomas touched her shoulder and said it was time to go.

"May I keep the book until I'm done reading it?" asked Ruby.

"Of course!" said Ms. Thomas, even more surprised than Ruby. "Oh Ruby, I think this is going to work out just fine for you. Would you like to come back to Mr. Monroes class again tomorrow?"

"Yes," said Ruby. "Please!"

As she held the book close, she whispered, "Sunny, you were right! You were so right! Thank you!"

11

Over the next few weeks, Ruby was moved into a general education Math class with Ms. Juno, Language Arts with Mr. Monroe, and Science with Mr. Randolf. She kept bringing her magic stones in her front pockets. When the room got too loud, she would gently touch her green stone and things would quiet down. If math became too difficult, she would tap on her blue stone and her mind would clear. When she had to write, her red stone always kept the ideas flowing from her brain to the paper.

And, of course, her yellow stone opened up her brain to a world of words. Suddenly, she could read and understand everything on the page.

She loved her new friendships. She and Lizzy officially became best friends. They walked to and from school, and they hung out after class and on weekends.

Ruby had a hard time remembering what her life had been like before she found her magic stones. She was so happy to have them.

On the last day of school, she was walking home with her friends. They talked about summer plans and what eighth grade would be like next year.

As Ruby said goodbye and headed towards her house, she was stopped. Her eyes were pulled toward the grass near her front door. There she saw a purple bag that looked an awful lot like her magic, red bag!

She bent down to pick it up.

Inside were four more stones. This time they were purple, orange, black and white.

She slipped them into her pocket and walked inside her house.

I wonder what they are, she thought, as she tucked them away in a box in her closet.

I wonder?

About The Author

Lori Werhane is the parent to one gifted child and two twice exceptional children (gifted and learning disabled with a splash of ADD and Autism-like struggles). She also spent three years working in a public middle school as a paraprofessional supporting children with severe/significant needs. While her background is in photography and creative arts, her immersion in special education over the last seven years has given her a unique perspective into the special education system, its professionals and most importantly children who struggle. Ms. Werhane lives near Denver, Colorado, with her husband, and three children. Her true passion is using her imagination for storytelling through her photography, blog and creative writing projects.

About The Publisher

Story Shares is a nonprofit focused on supporting the millions of teens and adults who struggle with reading by creating a new shelf in the library specifically for them. The ever-growing collection features content that is compelling and culturally relevant for teens and adults, yet still readable at a range of lower reading levels.

Story Shares generates content by engaging deeply with writers, bringing together a community to create this new kind of book. With more intriguing and approachable stories to choose from, the teens and adults who have fallen behind are improving their skills and beginning to discover the joy of reading. For more information, visit storyshares.org.

Easy to Read. Hard to Put Down.

Printed in the USA
CPSIA information can be obtained
at www.ICGtesting.com
JSHW021914240923
48796JS00012B/351

9 781642 611786